Beauty and the Beet

Adapted by
Karen Kreider

Illustrated by
Mark Marderosian
Jim Mitchell
Phil Ortiz
Jim Story
Don Williams

MALLARD
PRESS

Twin Books

It was a normal day at a normal research lab at St. Canard University—normal, that is, except for Dr. Reggie Bushroot, a scientist with a passion for plants. His two lab partners, Dr. Gary and Dr. Larson, were tossing around one of Reggie's potato experiments when *she* walked in—the ravishing Dr. Rhoda Dendron.

Reggie's heart fluttered as he watched her walk by. He was fumbling with his latest flower experiment when his boss, Dean Tightbill, walked in and announced that he would no longer pay for Reggie's plant experiments. Reggie was horrified. All his valuable research would be lost! But worst of all, he would probably never see Dr. Dendron again!

Later that night, as thunder and lightning crashed and flickered outside his greenhouse, Reggie strapped himself to an operating table. A tube ran from Reggie's arm to a small potted flower that lay strapped to another table. "Once I prove that my theories work, the Dean will have to let me come back." Reggie turned to the plant. "Ready?" he asked. "Here's to a better tomorrow!"

Reggie flipped the switch and the two tables rose towards the ceiling. The glass roof opened up. An antenna rose and caught a lightning bolt. Electricity zipped all around and jolted Reggie and the flower several feet off the tables.

7

Reggie was crushed the next morning when he awoke feeling normal. "My experiment is a failure!" he moaned.

But when he walked out of the greenhouse, the sun's rays hit him like a bolt of last night's lightning. The sun was feeding him nutrients the way it feeds plants. "It works!" he exclaimed gleefully. "Wow! Wait 'til the research department sees that my experiment is a success. They'll never look at me the same way again."

Then he noticed his hands were turning green. "Hmm. Could be a side effect," said Reggie. He shrugged. "Well, being green won't be so bad."

He practically skipped back to the lab. He didn't notice that leaves were sprouting out of his head.

By the time Reggie reached the lab, he was a full-blown salad bar. "It worked, everybody!" shouted Reggie.

But Dr. Gary and Dr. Larson weren't impressed. They just taunted him. "Reggie's a veggie! Reggie's a veggie!"

Humiliated, Reggie ran outside, stumbling on his plant feet.
"All I ever wanted was to make the world a better place to live,"
he sighed.

Tired and confused, Reggie looked around for a place to sit. A
flower sprang up behind him and formed a chair. He sat down,
mopping his brow with a leafy hand. "Thanks," he panted.

All at once, he leaped up. "How did that happen?" he gasped.

Then a tree branch offered him a drink of water, spilling it at Reggie's feet. His foot sucked up the water like a vacuum cleaner. "Ahh," sighed Reggie, contentedly. He looked from the tree to the flower chair. The plants could understand his thoughts! What a scientific breakthrough!

But his excitement passed quickly. "They'll just laugh at me again, in front of Rhoda," he groaned.

Reggie suddenly thought of another strategy. "Unless, of course, they have a little accident," he thought. "Hmm. This plant thing may not be so bad after all!"

That night, Dr. Gary and Dr. Larson were working late in the lab. As they huddled around the work table, two vines slithered through the door and wrapped around their legs.

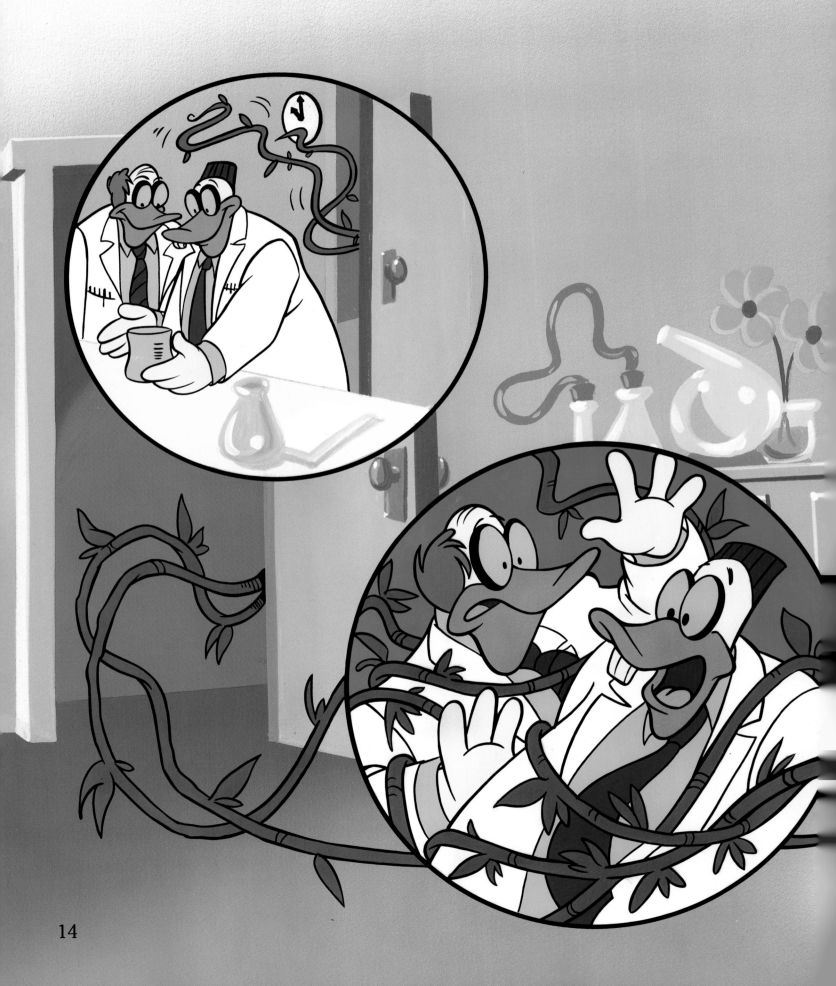

When the vines finished their task, there was nothing left of the two scientists but their forms made out of bushes.

It was a case for Darkwing Duck. "A classic case of revenge," declared Darkwing. "Dr. Reggie Bushroot's revenge."

Convinced that Bushroot's revenge wasn't complete, Darkwing and his loyal sidekick, Launchpad, busily hammered planks across all the windows in Dean Tightbill's office. After all, it was he who'd stopped Reggie's experiments.

"Let's see that big begonia try to get through this," Darkwing said proudly.

All at once, a giant tree crashed through the wall and grabbed Dean Tightbill. "Stop, you sizable sapling!" warned Darkwing. But the tree just stomped out of the building with the squirming dean hanging from a branch.

Darkwing sprang into action. He hollered to distract the tree. Tightbill fell out of the branches and ran away.

Reggie witnessed his plan being foiled. "You spoiled my fun," snarled Reggie. "Now I'm going to have to do to you what I did to them." With a thought, he commanded the tree to attack Darkwing and Launchpad.

As the tree loomed over them, Darkwing
quickly buzzed the leaves off the branches with
his buzz-saw cuff links. Meanwhile, the other
trees were helping Reggie escape by tossing him
from branch to branch.

Darkwing and Launchpad jumped onto the Ratcatcher and sped off after Reggie. Just as they were about to catch up to him, Reggie jumped on a vine that he signalled to grow. The Ratcatcher followed at full speed as the vine spiraled up higher and higher. Suddenly Darkwing and Launchpad found themselves performing the most daredevil stunts imaginable—loop-the-loops, corkscrew spirals, hairpin turns. Just when they thought their heads would never stop spinning, the Ratcatcher zoomed towards the ground.

"Aiii!" shrieked Darkwing.

"Yiii!" screamed Launchpad.

As Darkwing and Launchpad staggered away from the wreckage, Reggie said smugly, "That ought to teach you."

But Darkwing was no ordinary duck. He pulled out his ray gun. "Okay, Bushroot. The sprig is up."

Reggie raised his arms. But instead of surrendering, he created a thick forest around him.

Darkwing hacked away at the trees with his machete. But Reggie was gone! Looking down a freshly dug hole, Launchpad observed, "Looks like maybe Reggie decided to go back to his roots!" Darkwing just scowled.

Back at St. Canard University, Rhoda continued her work in the lab, all the while worrying about Dr. Bushroot. Suddenly Darkwing burst through the door, followed by Launchpad. They both looked tired and tattered. Rhoda rushed towards them. "Did you find Dr. Bushroot?" she asked. Launchpad nodded.

"Oooh, poor Reginald! I feel so sorry for him," sighed Rhoda.

"Are you kidding?" exclaimed Launchpad. "If it wasn't for D.W., we'd be side dishes at the salad bar!"

But Rhoda couldn't believe that Dr. Bushroot was capable of such horrible deeds.

Reggie overheard their entire conversation. "Reginald! She called me Reginald! Rhoda likes me!" he sighed.

Reggie was transformed from vengeance-crazed vegetable to passion fruit. With help from the trees and the bushes, he brushed off his tuxedo, trimmed his hair with hedge clippers and set off to declare his undying love.

Meanwhile, over at the lab, Darkwing was trying on a disguise of vine leaves to help snare Reggie when Rhoda interrupted him. "Mr. Darkwing, that is poison ivy," she said.

"Aahh! Eee! Oooh!" yelped Darkwing. "That explains this incredible itching sensation." There was a loud crash as he hit the table full of test tubes while trying to untangle himself.

Launchpad was amazed. "Hey, D.W., nice crash. And you didn't even have a plane!"

Suddenly two rose bushes burst through the door, rolling out a red carpet and tossing rose petals around the room.

"Dr. Bushroot!" gasped Rhoda as Reggie strutted in.

"Rhoda, my darling!" he cried, rushing towards her.

Darkwing jumped between them. "Not so fast, flower face," he said.

But Reggie was determined to leave with his lady love. "Spike will take care of you two," said Reggie. He ordered his Venus flytrap to attack. "Sic 'em, Spike!"

Chomping and slurping, Spike moved in on Darkwing and Launchpad. Reggie walked out, Rhoda struggling in his arms.

"Here, Spike! Here, boy!" coaxed Darkwing. He had to think fast. He grabbed a bone from a nearby hanging skeleton. "Go get it, boy!" he called as he heaved the bone across the room.

Eager as a puppy, the Venus flytrap bounded after the bone. But just as Darkwing and Launchpad prepared to make their getaway, Spike rushed back and spat out the bone at their feet.

"Er, good boy, Spike," said Darkwing. "Now go fetch!" He tossed the bone out the window. Spike followed.

"Whew! Thanks, D.W.," sighed Launchpad, relieved. "I thought we were plant food there for a second."

Darkwing headed for the door. "C'mon, Launchpad. We've got some gardening to do!"

Later that night at the greenhouse, Reggie was completing the final steps to make Rhoda his bride. Outside, lightning flashed and thunder boomed. Rhoda struggled to free herself from the same table where Reggie had been transformed. Another quivering flower lay strapped to the other table, ready to sacrifice its petals for Reggie's dream date.

"I'm afraid your gardening days are over," said Reggie, waving his hand at a tree. The tree lurched towards Darkwing and grabbed the weed cutter.

"That's it!" cried Darkwing. "Now we're going to do some serious weeding!" He darted off and returned driving a power mower. "Hi-ho, slicer! Away!"

Darkwing chased Reggie, who hid behind a pot of lilies. As the mower loomed closer, Reggie pulled back the lilies and let go a cloud of pollen right in Darkwing's face!

"Achoo!" With a violent sneeze, Darkwing fell off the mower.

Meanwhile, the glass panels in the roof swung open as Rhoda and the flower approached the top. The storm got worse. "Help! Darkwing Duck, hellllp!" screamed Rhoda.

Darkwing's eyes narrowed. "Let's get dangerous!" he hissed.

"I'll give you dangerous!" Reggie cried as he stepped over to a large cactus. The cactus bent back and let its needles fly. Dodging the thorny missiles, Darkwing used them as a ladder and began to climb towards the struggling Rhoda.

The lightning was zipping all around her. Just as a streak of lightning reached toward the antenna, Darkwing leaped onto a thick, dangling electrical cord. "Yiiiii!" he screamed, as he pushed off from his perch, clinging to the cord. With a loud crackling sound, the plug ripped away from the wall.

"No!" cried Reggie as he watched the operating tables lowering to the ground. "You're ruining everything!"

Darkwing slid off the cord, landed on the mower, and took off after Reggie. "Time to toss a little salad!" he cracked.

Reggie turned to run as the mower came directly at him. "Stop!" yelled Reggie, throwing pots and tables in the mower's path. But Darkwing steered the mower right through the obstacles. He soared over an upturned table and loomed like a shadow over Reggie.

42

Whirrr! went the mower.

"Succotash!" crowed Darkwing.

Leaves were scattered everywhere as the mower sputtered
to a stop.

Meanwhile, Launchpad had finally pulled the pumpkin off his head. "Yuck!" he sputtered.

Darkwing rushed to free Rhoda from the operating table. "Oh, thank you, Mr. Darkwing!" she said.

"All in a day's work," said Darkwing. "I merely exercised my famous deductive abilities and my lightning-fast reflexes. Right, Launchpad?"

"Oh . . . right, D.W.," said Launchpad, picking pumpkin seeds out of his hair.

And they all chuckled merrily as the crimefighters closed another incredible case.

But outside the greenhouse, in a soft, moist flower bed,
sunlight was streaming down on a little cabbage starting to grow.
"Ahh, my own little place in the sun," said Reggie Bushroot.
"Before they know it, I'll be back on my roots again!"